DISNEY

Lady and the TRAMP

Adapted by

Brooke Vitale

Illustrated by the

Disney Storybook Art Team

𝒟ISNEP PRESS

Los Angeles • New York

First Box Set Edition, September 2017
1 3 5 7 9 10 8 6 4 2
ISBN 978-1-368-00671-2
FAC-025393-17167
Printed in China
For more Disney Press fun, visit www.disneybooks.com

On Christmas Eve,
Jim Dear gives his wife a gift.
It is a puppy!
Darling names her Lady.

Lady has two friends.
Their names are
Jock and Trusty.
They live next door.

Lady shows Jock and Trusty
her new collar.
She is very
proud of it.

Lady talks to
Jock and Trusty.
She is happy.
A baby is coming!

A dog named Tramp
hears Lady talking.
Tramp has no home.
Jock says he is trouble.

Soon the baby comes.
Jim Dear and Darling are happy.
Lady is happy.
She loves the baby.

Jim Dear and Darling
go on a trip.
Aunt Sarah comes
to watch the baby.

Aunt Sarah does not like Lady.
She thinks Lady is trouble.
She takes Lady to the pet store.
She buys her a muzzle.

Lady is scared.
She runs away.
She is chased by
a pack of dogs.

Tramp saves Lady
from the dogs.
He helps her
take off the muzzle.

Tramp takes Lady to
his favorite restaurant.
They share a meal.
They fall in love.

The next morning,
Tramp shows Lady
how to chase chickens.
A farmer chases them.

Lady is caught by
the dogcatcher.
She is taken
to the pound.

The dogcatcher
calls Aunt Sarah.
She gets Lady.
She brings Lady home.

Aunt Sarah is
mad at Lady.
She chains her to
the doghouse.

Tramp comes to see Lady.
Lady will not speak to him.
She thinks he left her behind.

Tramp is sorry.
He thought she was
running behind him.

Tramp goes away.
Lady sees a rat.
It climbs into
the baby's room.

Lady barks at the rat.
Aunt Sarah thinks she
is being bad.
She yells at Lady.

Tramp hears Lady barking.
He tries to catch the rat.

Lady breaks her chain.
She runs into
the baby's room.

Aunt Sarah hears
Lady and Tramp.
She thinks they are
hurting the baby.

She locks Lady
in the closet.
She calls the dogcatcher
to get Tramp.

Jim Dear and Darling come home.
Lady shows Jim Dear the rat.
Jim Dear knows he must
go save Tramp.

Jock and Trusty help.
They make the
dogcatcher's cart
tip over.

Jim Dear saves Tramp.
He brings him home.

Tramp is a hero.
He saved the baby.

Christmas comes again.
Lady and Tramp have
their own babies.
They are happy.